"THAT'S ONE SMALL STEP FOR A MAN, ONE GIANT LEAP FOR MANKIND."
×××NEIL A. ARMSTRONG

"A THIN MAN RAN; MAKES A LARGE STRIDE; LEFT PLANET, PINS FLAG ON MOON. ON TO MARS!"

For my fine family, who brings my life infamy.
(Of course this includes the Ragen range.) —M. S.

A dear grin for Gardiner. —A. M.

An anagram of thanks to our wonderful editor Victoria Rock at:
*Chronicle Books, Second street, San Francisco, USA,*
*the classic canon of editor Rock bears consensus.*

Text © 2013 by Mark Shulman.
Illustrations © 2013 by Adam McCauley.

Library of Congress Cataloging-in-Publication Data available.
ISBN 978-1-4521-0914-5

Manufactured in China.

Book design by Cynthia Wigginton and Sara Gillingham Studio.
Typeset in Archive Tilt, Cross Stitch Simple, Faywood,
Graphique Pro, Knockout, Learning Curve, Matchwood, and Ultinoid.
The illustrations in this book were rendered in mixed media.

10 9 8 7 6 5 4 3 2 1

Chronicle Books LLC
680 Second Street, San Francisco, California 94107

Chronicle Books—we see things differently. Become part
of our community at www.chroniclekids.com.

# ANN
## AND
# NAN
## ARE
# ANAGRAMS

## A MIXED-UP WORD DILEMMA

By MARK SHULMAN

Illustrated by ADAM McCAULEY

chronicle books · san francisco

My name is

**ROBERT OR BERT.**

Please, don't call me Bob.
That's a whole other story.

Word problems run
in my family.

Then **SHE WHISPERED** like a **WISE SHEPHERD:**

"Anagrams are easy to **SPOT**

but hard to **STOP.**

Now take the **TOPS**

off the **POTS**

hurry to the **POST** office,

Elizabeth Hazelbite
13579 Bad Velour Boulevard
Ant Moan, Montana 59137

and bring me your **AUNT**.

She's **A NUT**."

POST? POT S?

TOPS? SPOT?

STOP!

Her mixed-up **WORDS** hit me like a **SWORD.**

Poor Grandma!

What a **VILE, EVIL** way to **LIVE**. And I don't even *have* an aunt.

How could I RESCUE and SECURE my granny?

**I RAN** like **RAIN** to warn **MOM** and **DAD**,
but they were acting **MOD and MAD**.

And my sisters, Ann and Nan?

*O no!*

ANN and NAN

are anagrams!

I SHOT MY COOL and ran TO MY SCHOOL. The SCHOOLMASTER was in THE CLASSROOM teaching VOWELS to WOLVES and feeding PRESENTS to SERPENTS.

AeiOU
oUeiA
ELEVEN PLUS TWO
= TWELVE PLUS ONE
GOLD ROACHES
GRADE SCHOOL

I **FLED** to a **FIELD**, which was QUITE QUIET.
I watched a BUTTERFLY FLUTTER BY
just BELOW my ELBOW.

WINGS SWING!

It was the NICEST INSECT, but it couldn't
end this MOOD of DOOM.

What could I DO BUT DOUBT?

How could I bring Grandma a nutty aunt I don't have?

THE ANSWER just WASN'T HERE.

I needed A WAY
to get AWAY.

What were my
BEST BETS?

Not my **RACE CAR**— it needed **CAR CARE**.

Not my **TRAIN**— **IT RAN IN TAR.**

Not my OCEAN CANOE— it would LEAK in the LAKE.

And a **SUBMARINE BURIES MAN** under water.

Not happening!

Then, DOWN THE STREET in THE DESERT TOWN,
what I ~~SAW WAS~~ . . . a DINER, IN RED.

I was **SILENT**,
so I could **LISTEN**.

I turned the **KNOB**.
There was a **BONK**.

I opened the **DOOR UP**.
**P.U.! ODOR!**

I took two **STEPS—PESTS!**
I was in NATURE'S RAT RESTAURANT!
I dropped a **PLATE** and **LEAPT** away.
UCKY! YUCK! *This* is why **EXITS EXIST**.

At long last, I found a real place to EAT.

So I ATE and had TEA.

That's when I found **THIS BRIDGE**
and tried to look on the **BRIGHT SIDE.**

There was no way I could
bring Grandma Reagan an **AUNT**,
so I brought her a . . .

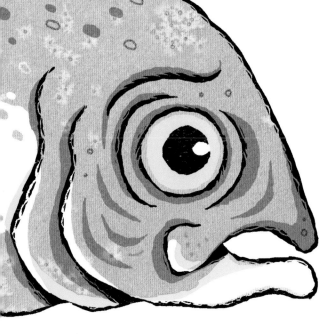

# TUNA.

"THAT'S ONE SMALL STEP FOR A MAN, ONE GIANT LEAP FOR MANKIND."
~NEIL A. ARMSTRONG

"A THIN MAN RAN; MAKES A LARGE STRIDE; LEFT PLANET, PINS FLAG ON MOON. ON TO MARS!"